GORDON'S GOT A SNOOKIE

story by
LISA SHANAHAN

pictures by
WAYNE HARRIS

ALLEN & UNWIN

**For Max, Toby, Connor, Keats, Ben,
Dan, Mitchell, Tristan, Bryn and Riley — L.S.**

For Pete, Donna, Alice and Gary — W.H.

First published in 2002

Copyright © Text, Lisa Shanahan 2002
Copyright © Illustrations, Wayne Harris 2002

Allen & Unwin
83 Alexander Street
Crows Nest NSW 2065 Australia
Phone: (61 2) 8425 0100
Fax: (61 2) 9906 2218
Email: info@allenandunwin.com
Web: www.allenandunwin.com

National Library of Australia
Cataloguing-in-Publication entry:

Shanahan, Lisa.
Gordon's got a snookie.

For children aged 3-7 years.
ISBN 1 86508 691 6.

I. Gorilla — Juvenile fiction. I. Harris, Wayne. II. Title.

A823.3

The illustrations for this book were created digitally
Cover and text design by Monkeyfish
Set in Highlander by Monkeyfish

Printed in China by Everbest Printing Co.

10 9 8 7 6 5 4 3 2

One evening, the animals
of the zoo could not sleep.

"Gordon is coming!" cried the giraffe to the tiger.

"Gordon is coming!" roared the tiger to the seal.

"Gordon is coming!"
barked the seal to
the yak.

"Gordon is coming!"
babbled the yak
to the gnu.

"Whoopee! Whoo-hoo! Yee-ha! Yippety-whoo-hee! Gordon is coming! Gordon is coming!"

The yak stopped dancing and gazed at the gnu.

"Who is Gordon?" he asked.

"Don't you know?" asked the gnu.

"If I knew," asked the yak, "would I be asking you?"

"He's a gorilla," said the gnu. "The new top boy. The big silverback. They're flying him in from a zoo overseas, so that he can take care of the girls."

"Hoo-whee!" said the yak.

The girls were wide awake.
The air was hot and steamy.

"I hope he's big,"
said Gidget.

"I hope he's strong,"
said Doris.

"I hope he's hairy,"
said Delilah.

And eventually they fell asleep
and dreamt lovely dreams about
a big, strong, hairy gorilla.

The next morning, the gorillas
met Gordon for the first time.
Gordon grinned at the girls.
He flexed his pecs.
He bulged his biceps.
He pummelled his chest and roared.

"R

But the baby gorillas laughed and laughed.

"Look!" screeched Abu, the smallest gorilla.

"Gordon's got a snookie. Gordon's got a snookie!"

"Gordon's got a snookie!"
cried the giraffe
to the tiger.

"Gordon's got a snookie!"
roared the tiger
to the seal.

"Gordon's got a snookie!"
barked the seal
to the yak.

"Gordon's got a snookie!" babbled the yak to the gnu.
"Gordon's got a snookie! Boo hoo! Waah haa baa!"

The yak stopped dancing
and gazed at the gnu.

"What's a snookie?" he
whispered.

"Don't you know?" asked
the gnu.

"If I knew," hissed the yak,
"would I be asking you?"

"A snookie," said the gnu,
"is a cuddly, a comforter, a
blanky-blanky."

"What do you use it for?"
asked the yak.

"You carry it with you
wherever you go," said the gnu,
"and whenever you feel
lonely or scared or you miss your
mummy, you hug it tight."

"You are in the know!"
said the yak.

The animals laughed themselves
silly over Gordon and his snookie.
The hyena laughed so much
he was carted off to hospital.

The gorillas were embarrassed and ashamed.

"Do you want to squeeze
my muscles?" Gordon asked.

"No thanks,"
mumbled Gidget.

"What about we go for a
climb?" Gordon called.

"Not today,"
muttered Doris.

"My coat could do with
a bit of nitpicking," Gordon beamed.

"I'm not hungry,"
sighed Delilah.

And they turned their backs
on Gordon and ignored him.

Gordon could not understand it.
He tried his best. But, before long,
he was the loneliest animal in the
whole zoo. And the lonelier he
became, the harder he hugged his
snookie. And the harder he hugged
his snookie, the more the other
animals laughed. And the more the
other animals laughed, the more the
other gorillas ignored him. And the
more the other gorillas ignored him,
the lonelier he became. And the
lonelier he became, of course, the
harder he hugged his snookie.

Soon he was so lonely, he couldn't move.

One morning, while Gordon was sleeping, Abu fell into the moat.

"Aaaa-eeee!"
screamed Abu.
"Mumma!"

But the water was deep and dark, and even the biggest and strongest gorillas can't swim.

"Mumma!"
cried Abu.
"Mumma!"

Gidget stretched out a stick.
Doris held out a branch.
Delilah tossed in a piece of rope.
But nothing could reach the smallest gorilla.

"Mumma!"

"Help!" wailed Abu's mother. "Help!"

Gordon woke up. When he saw Abu
thrashing in the water, something
inside him boiled.

"WRAAA-OOGH!"
he roared.
"WRAAA-OOGH!"

He leapt to his feet.
He snatched up his snookie.
With a mighty rip, he tore
it in two. He tied the pieces
together and swung it
into the moat.

"Grab the snookie!"

cried Gordon, as one end smacked into the water.

"Grab the snookie!"
shouted the giraffe
and the tiger.

"Grab the snookie!"
bellowed the seal
and the gnu.

"Grab the snookie!"
gushed the gorillas.

"Why does he have to
grab the snookie?"
asked the yak.

"Stop your yackety-yak!"
said the gnu. "And watch!"

Abu grabbed the snookie

and Gordon dragged him in.

As soon as Abu reached
the bank, his mother
hugged him tight.

Gordon untied the
snookie and wrung it out.
Then he wrapped Abu in the
biggest piece.

"There you go," he said,
wiping the tears from the
smallest gorilla's eyes.

The animals of the zoo were still and silent.

"Whoopee!
Whoo-hoo!"
cheered the yak
suddenly,
dancing about.

"Whoopee!
Whoo-hoo!"
cried the animals
of the zoo.

"Yippety-
whoo-hee!"

Gordon grinned. He flexed his pecs. He bulged
his biceps. He pummelled his chest and roared.

"You are so big!"
said Gidget.
"I want to squeeze
your muscles!"

"You are so strong!"
said Doris.
"I want to climb
with you always."

"You are so hairy!"

said Delilah.
"I want to nitpick
you forever!"

From that day on,
Gordon was never
lonely again.

And neither were any
of the other animals.
For whenever they
felt lonely, or scared,
or missed their mummies,
they each hugged tight
their very own snookie.